GILGO B

CW00959627

a Mary MacIn

Maureen

MAUREEN ANNE MEEHAN

GILGO BEACH,

Copyright © 2025 by Maureen Anne Meehan

ISBN: 979-8-3484-7035-7

E-book ISBN: 979-8-3484-7036-4

All rights reserved. No part of this publication may be reproduced, distributed, or transmitted in any form or by any means, including photocopying, recording, or other electronic or mechanical methods, without the prior written permission of the publisher and/or the author, except in the case of brief quotations embodied in critical reviews and other noncommercial uses permitted by copyright law.

The views expressed in this book are solely those of the author and do not necessarily reflect the views of the publisher, and the publisher hereby disclaims any responsibility for them.

www. maureenmeehanbooks.com

info@maureenmeehan.com

Table of Contents

AUTHOR'S DEDICATION

Gilgo Beach, a Mary MacIntosh novel is dedicated to the victims of the serial killer, Rex Heuermann. He is accused of killing at least eight people and has been indicted for the murders of Melissa Barthelemy, Megan Waterman, Amber Costello, Maureen Brainard-Barnes, Jessica Taylor, Sandra Costilla, and Valerie Mack. It is possible that he is responsible for a two-year-old baby's murder and that of an Asian man. The book is dedicated to all known and unknown victims of the Gilgo Beach murders.

Logan Crawford got recognition for reminding me of this serial killer during our recent interview on his podcast, *Spotlight on America*. Logan is a man of many talents and my hat is tipped to him for encouraging me to craft another Mary MacIntosh novel.

AUTHOR'S NOTE

2025 is a pivotal year for me as I am selling all content to major motion picture and/or streaming services for both the Mary MacIntosh series as well as my dating series starting with *60 Dates in Six Months (with a Broken Neck)*. In addition to the desire to make movies, I have also pivoted to podcast and have released a few true crime podcasts for *Only the Truth* which so far remain focused on the Mary MacIntosh series as the novels are fictionalized versions of true crime. Podcasts are much easier than crafting novels and require far less time, allowing time to focus more this year on family, friends, and careers.

New challenges are fun and keep the brain focused and sharp.

Chapter 1

Rex Heuermann, a 60-year-old architect from Long Island, New York, was a married man with two children, and by all accounts, an intelligent stand-out career and family man. One would never venture to guess that he would be arrested and arraigned for multiple counts of murder in the first degree.

When Mary MacIntosh received the call from FBI profiler, John Douglas, about the case, she was surprised that it had taken law enforcement so long to catch this serial killer. Mac and John talked at length about the facts of the case, and John asked Mac for assistance the FBI believed that there were several more victims of the Giglo Beach murders, and the FBI wanted her help.

Mac had been keeping a low profile after the Tooth Fairy Killer case and was focused on her four children. She had permanently moved out of the family home and had purchased another home near the Sheridan, Wyoming fairgrounds. She wanted to be close enough that the four children could walk or ride their bikes to her home, and she and Burg had agreed to share custody in their divorce.

"Mac, we really need your help," John pleaded. "We've uncovered at least eight victims so far, but we fear that there are many others out there.

He left behind so much DNA at these crime scenes, and as meticulous as he was about planning the murders, he was pretty sloppy in the execution. It's like he was an architect in the planning and then became a ruthless monster in the killing."

"The kids are in a good place post-divorce and are settled into a routine of every other week with Burg and me, and Burg has become less clingy. He's come to the resolution that I simply can't forgive what happened during the Tooth Fairy Killer case. I've moved on. I'm not dating anyone, but I've heard that he is. I think it is healthy for him to date. It was time for him to move forward," Mac explained.

"If they are settled and in a good place, can you fly to New York on your week without the kids and meet us there? We want to share the file with you and hire you to consult on the Giglo Beach murders," John said.

"Can I discuss it with the children? If they are okay with it, then the answer is yes. I have not worked since the Tooth Fairy Killer case, and I bought a home and could use the income," Mac said.

"I pray that the kids don't mind you being absent for one week. You probably have not had a vacation since prior to the divorce," John said.

"True. I've only gone skiing and camping etc. with the kids. I have not gone anywhere just for me."

"Call me after you talk with the kids. I'm hoping for a positive response."

"Will do," she said. Within a few minutes, she received an email from the FBI regarding the Giglo Beach murders. She clicked on the file and started to read. It was a fascinating tale indeed.

Chapter 2

"John, the kids are okay with me being gone next week starting Sunday as long as I return the following Saturday morning in time for their respective sports," Mac said.

"Great news. I'll send a driver to collect you at JFK and bring you to the hotel in Times Square," John said.

"Sounds good. I was perusing the file that your team sent, and this man is accused of outlandishly peculiar crimes. It appears that he started killing in 2010 or earlier and that he primarily focused on young women working as sex workers."

"Yes, the first arrest in Manhattan was for the murders of Melissa Barthelemy, Megan Waterman, and Amber Costello in July 2023, but DNA evidence has tied him potentially to murders prior to 2010," John said.

"Looks like he was charged again in January 2024 with the murder of Maureen Brainard-Barnes, and then arraigned and charged in June 2024 with the murders of Jessica Taylor and Sandra Costilla," Mac said.

"In December 2024 he was indicted for the 2000 murder of Valerie Mack, so this guy has been killing for a very long time," John noted.

"How did it take law enforcement so long to catch this guy? It seemed like he was leading such a double life as the faithful husband and doting father of two kids, yet, he somehow managed to sneak away from the family with enough time to kill a lot of people," Mac said.

"He was hiding in plain sight," John said. "What remains so odd with this guy is that he was meticulous in planning the murders, and then so sloppy in the execution. That is not typically what we see as profilers. They are usually meticulous on all accounts or sloppy on all accounts, but a mixed bag is very new to us at the FBI. Folks are scratching their heads over this one. The issue is that we now think that there are more victims, and that is why we need you. With your profiler experience, and your legal cleverness, combined with your degree in psychology, we need to delve into this man's motives and try to peel away at his psychological background to try to determine if other missing persons or murders in New York can be tied to Rex Heuermann," John said.

"Why did it take so long for law enforcement to link Heuermann to the crimes through various means, including DNA evidence obtained from items he discarded? They found burner phone records, internet searches, Mitochondrial DNA testing from a discarded pizza crust, and a burlap used to wrap one of the victims. That seems like a lot of evidence not to have detected this guy long before now," Mac said.

"He isn't in CODIS, that's why. He led a squeaky clean life and had never been arrested before, so the DNA left behind at multiple crime scenes was not linked to him because we didn't have his DNA," John explained.

"Makes sense," Mac said.

"I'm grateful that you are going to arrive in New York on Sunday, and we can brainstorm in person. Looking forward to working with you again," John said as they ended the call.

Chapter 3

When Mac landed at JFK in New York, a car was awaiting her at the airport and whisked her to the hotel in Times Square. John was waiting for her in their "war room" where they would hunker down for the week and work on the case.

"Prosecutors from the District Attorney's Office have revealed to us at the FBI that Heuermann allegedly created detailed 'planning documents' outlining his methods for committing the murders and disposing of the bodies. These documents were found on his computer that they confiscated from his home office," John explained. "Note that the victims were primarily young female sex workers. However, the remains discovered of a two-year-old girl and an Asian man indicate a broader victim profile. That is where we step in. We believe that there are more victims out there in light of this new discovery regarding the baby and the Asian male."

"Doesn't that seem terribly odd that he has detailed plans for the female sex workers but there is no plan for the baby and the Asian man?" Mac asked.

"Yes, that's why we are now pivoting to a broader victim profile and reexamining the case. We are looking into a broader spectrum of possible victims of the Gilgo Beach Killer, as we are calling him at the FBI," John said.

"Heuermann has pleaded not guilty to all charges and remains in custody awaiting trial. His defense attorneys have recently filed motions to exclude certain DNA evidence from the trial, challenging the reliability of the techniques used," John said.

"So the investigation into the Gilgo Beach murders is ongoing, with authorities continuing to seek information related to other unidentified victims such as the 'Asian Doe' whose details were recently released to the public in hopes of gathering more information?" Mac asked.

"As of January 16, 2025, Rex Heuermann was charged with the murder of Valerie Mack, bringing the total number of his alleged victims to seven, confirmed, but we believe that there are many more," John said.

"Looks like Valerie Mack was a 24-year-old woman who worked as the case, then there is a large gap in victims from 2000 to 2010, which leads me to believe that there are many more victims out there," Mac said.

John nodded in agreement, watching Mac quickly get up to speed on the case.

"Melissa Taylor's partial remains were discovered in Manorville, New York, in November 2000, with further remains found near Gilgo Beach in 2011. Investigators linked Heuermann to Valerie Mack a/k/a Melissa Taylor through DNA evidence, including hairs from his daughter and estranged wife found on Mack's remains," John added. "On January 7, 2025, Heuermann's attorneys filed a motion requesting the exclusion of expert testimony related to nuclear DNA results from hairs found at six crime scenes. They argued that the technique used is not reliable, but you know better than anyone that nuclear DNA is extremely reliable. Therefore, it is highly doubtful that the attorneys will be successful in dismissing this evidence."

"I'm reading that Suffolk County District Attorney Ray Tierney, who has been instrumental in the investigation, announced his reelection campaign on January 7, 2025. He highlighted his office's achievements, including the establishment of a specialized task force for the Gilgo Beach murders, which led to Heuermann's arrest. According to the New York Post, pretrial hearings for Heuermann are set to commence soon," Mac said.

"The FBI is thrilled with these recent developments as they indicate ongoing legal proceedings and efforts to address the Gilgo Beach murders, with the case against Rex Heuermann progressing through the legal system," John said. "We remain hopeful that a trial date will be set soon."

"During a court appearance on December 17, 2024, Judge Timothy Mazzei expressed the intention to establish a trial date at the next hearing, scheduled for February 2025 according to CBS News," Mac said. "The prosecution has indicated that the extensive volume of evidence may impact the timeline for setting a definitive trial date."

"While Heuermann has been charged in connection with seven of these cases, authorities continue to investigate the remaining unidentified victims to determine if there are any connections to Heuermann or other suspects," John added.

9

"I guess that's where I come in," Mac said. "You are asking that I assist the FBI with the ongoing investigation which aims to provide closure for all victims and their families."

"Precisely why you are here," John said.

Chapter 4

"After a good night of sleep in this loud city of 24/7 sirens," Mac said sarcastically, "I am ready to dig in."

"I am ready to brainstorm with you," John replied. "It's quite obvious that Rex Heuermann led a dual life of a seemingly normal family man who was hiding a deep-rooted angry life toward women he may have viewed as unethical."

"I find his patterns to be most curious," Mac said. "It seems like he might have committed these murders in his wife's absence. I think when she traveled on business, he left the kids unattended in the night and he slinked out of the family home hunting for sex workers to lure and kill."

"What makes you think that he did this when he wife was away?"

"It's logical. She would notice him sneaking out in the middle of the night. Women are notoriously light sleepers once they have children. I think she would have been awoken by him getting out of bed at night. Therefore, the logical conclusion is that he waited for her to be away from the home, which afforded him the opportunity to commit heinous acts of violence," Mac replied.

"I see. It's possible. We can't prove it because we don't know when most of these murders happened. We have no timeline. However, I can follow the logic of what you are suggesting," John said.

"Has the wife agreed to be interviewed and/or deposed?"

"No. She's asserting the husband/wife defense that entitles her to not give witness against her spouse," John said.

"Smart on her part, but as a mother of a daughter, I would think it would behoove her to cooperate with the law. If she doesn't, I think it makes her look suspicious and perhaps complicit in the acts, or at least willing to give him a possible alibi. She won't share her calendar as to when she traveled on business?" Mac asked.

"No. She refuses."

"Let's subpoena her work file. It is perfectly acceptable to ask for her employer's cooperation. What do we know about her place of work?" Mac asked.

"I'll ask the FBI legal team to have a paralegal issue the subpoena and to schedule a deposition in conjunction with the production of business records," John said. "To be honest, our team has not thought of that. It is a great idea. This is exactly why we need you on our team, Mac. You outwit and outsmart the FBI's legal team routinely."

"Flattery gets you everywhere with me," Mac said, as she tucked her No. 2 pencil behind her ear. Pulling her long auburn hair back at the same time.

John had aged over the years that she had been working with him. He was long past retirement age, but he loved his job so much that he had no intention of retiring, and the FBI director was thrilled to have such a great profiler mind still interested in pursuing justice.

John had commented to Mac more than once that she looked the same as she looked the day she graduated from law school. There was a picture on her office desk in Wyoming of Mac proudly holding her law degree with her mom smiling beside her with a grin from ear to ear. Mac still had her long, wavy auburn hair and deep-set honey brown eyes with a slim figure and a brimming grin.

"I'm not flattering you. I'm being honest. You've been here less than 24 hours, and you have already made a keen suggestion that no one else had thought about."

"It's simply logical that we would focus on his spouse. Also, since this has been going on for a long time, we need to look closely at the search warrant for their Long Island home and see what was discovered, and whether the FBI needs an additional warrant to continue the search. I have a feeling that he collected 'badges of honor' or 'tokens' of his victims. I have a hunch that perhaps one of his kids stumbled onto one or more of his 'trophies' and that his kids must have had some kind of exposure to his crimes. He was hiding in plain sight at work, at home, with his family, and I think that they knew more than they have revealed. Have the adult children been noticed for deposition?" Mac inquired.

"No, we didn't notice their deposition, nor did any other law enforcement. We think that it might look bad, and we know that his defense team would file motions to block this discovery," John said.

"It might look bad to depose them. I see your point. But we can serve them with written discovery, particularly requests for admission. Even if the defense lawyers file a motion to quash, we can file a motion to compel. There is no defense for the children not to admit or deny what they know. They are adults. Even if defense attorneys file for a protective order, I don't think that the judge will grant it. This is a high-profile case with likely other victims out there," Mac said.

"Okay, I will ask our legal team to proceed and prepare the written discovery," John agreed.

"I want to see it first before it is served. I've been a criminal defense lawyer and a prosecutor, and I believe that I am an expert in written discovery," Mac said, in a tone that was not braggy.

"Understood. I will instruct the team to send it to you first to review and revise before it goes out," John said.

Chapter 5

"Mac, I would like to introduce you to a New York Times journalist that I highly respect. This is Jayson Saunders, and he has been covering the Gilgo Beach murders for years," John said in the lobby of their hotel as he shook Jayson's hand. Mac's jaw visibly dropped, gazing at this stunning man who was wearing a handsome grey sweater, black creased slacks and a Guess jacket that hugged his trim frame nicely. She suddenly wished that she would have put on a little makeup and not had her hair up in a messy bun.

"Nice to meet you," Jayson said as he reached over to shake Mac's hand.

"The pleasure is mine," Mac blurted out before she could contain herself. She blushed with embarrassment. Something had come over her and she had little butterflies in her tummy. She nervously kept talking. "I am just getting up to speed on this case, and perhaps you can fill in the gaps for me."

"Sure," Jayson said as he escorted them into the hotel restaurant where they were to have dinner together and discuss the Gilgo Beach murders. He walked behind her with his hand lightly guiding her to a booth in the back of the steakhouse.

After they were seated and exchanged some small talk before focusing on the facts of the case. This was when she learned that he grew up in Bozeman, Montana, and attended Montana State University and earned his undergraduate degree in communications, his master's degree in psychology, and his Ph.D. in journalism. He had an impressive resume and an even more impressive career.

Mac downloaded him on her education and career as both a criminal defense attorney and a prosecutor before pivoting to consulting with the FBI with John.

"I'm impressed," Jayson said. "You have covered a lot of ground professionally."

"It's been a fun ride," Mac said with sincerity and pride. "I'm enjoying the most working with John. He's the consummate professional and has taught me a lot about profiling a case."

"He's the best of the best and the FBI is lucky that he hasn't retired. If the case can be cracked, John will be at the helm," Jayson said.

"Except for the Zodiac killer," John said with a certain level of disappointment in his tone.

"Tell me something that you have discovered that I won't see in the FBI file," Mac asked.

"There's a lot that I have uncovered that you won't see in their files," Jayson said.

"For example, I've done an extensive analysis of Rex Heuermann's personal and professional history and I have learned that he's had a darker, more twisted life than most are aware, and it helps explain his motive to kill."

"Do tell," Mac said. She was intrigued.

"First of all, he hated his wife and she hated him," Jayson said. "It was not a good marriage. Add to that, it is questionable whether he had a degree as an architect. He was good at what he did as one. Don't get me wrong, but I can find where he was educated. What's the kicker is that he had a hidden history of abuse and trauma dating back to his childhood which I believe fueled his desire to kill. I'm trying to determine whether his mother was a sex worker, or if she was simply neglectful or abusive, but there is a layer here that needs to be unveiled psychologically before his trial. I think it will explain the motive."

"That is intense," Mac said. "That psychological profile is very similar to that of the Tooth Fairy Killer."

"Exactly," John said.

"We have to decipher his motive to kill," Jayson said.

"It has to be deeply rooted in his formative years, as he is meticulous in the planning of these murders," Mac said.

"He has detailed outlines on his computer, which demonstrate premeditation. That is why his defense team continues to file motion after motion, but ultimately, they know that they are going to lose and that he's going to be convicted of multiple counts of murder in the first degree. The only decision will be whether the prosecutor goes for the death penalty, or life in prison without the possibility of parole."

"Based on the number of victims, which we are unclear of as of yet, and the premeditation, the FBI is hoping to convince the prosecutor to go for the death penalty. That is what Ted Bundy received and ultimately was put to death in Florida. Rodney Alcala as the Dating Game Killer also got the death penalty in California but based on California's policy of not enforcing the death penalty, Alcala died of natural causes in prison," John said.

"As a journalist investigating this case for years, I'm hoping for the death penalty," Jayson said.

"In Wyoming, it would be a no-brainer," Mac added.

"Same in Montana where I grew up," Jayson said.

"It's hard to say in New York, but one thing I think we can all agree, Rex Heuermann will never see the light of day again," John said with a sense of conviction.

Chapter 6

"What time is the press conference?" Mac asked John.

"I believe the FBI scheduled one for us with Jayson Saunders present this morning at 10 o'clock. It will be held on the courthouse steps where the case will be tried," John said.

The Suffolk County Court in Riverhead, New York is part of the Suffolk County court system, which handles both civil and criminal cases. The building is located in the town of Riverhead, serving as a central hub for legal proceedings in the county. The courthouse is designed to accommodate various legal processes, including high-profile criminal trials such as Heuermann's. It features multiple courtrooms equipped with modern facilities to ensure the smooth conduct of judicial proceedings. Security measures are stringent, especially during cases that attract significant public and media attention.

In Heuermann's case, the court has been actively managing pre-trial motions and hearings. For instance, his attorneys have filed motions to exclude certain DNA evidence, leading to scheduled hearings to determine the admissibility of this evidence at trial. Additionally, the District Attorney's office has faced challenges in meeting court-imposed deadlines due to resource constraints, highlighting the complexities involved in prosecuting such a case.

The Suffolk County Court continues to play a pivotal role in the administration of justice for this case, balancing the demands of a fair trial with the logistical challenges presented by the volume of evidence and public interest.

The case is being presided over by Judge Timothy Mazzei who has been actively managing the proceedings, including setting ambitious deadlines for evidence discovery and expressing a desire to establish a trial date.

In a recent development, Judge Mazzei ruled that Heuermann must submit a cheek swab for further DNA analysis, a decision that underscores his commitment to ensuring a thorough examination of the evidence. Judge Mazzei's proactive approach aims to balance the complexities of the case with the need for a timely trial, reflecting his dedication to the judicial process.

Judge Mazzei has presided over several other high-profile cases, including the Donatali O'Mahony Case in 2020. Judge Mazzei sentenced Donatila O'Mahony in March 2023 to 25 years to life in prison for the second-degree murder of Lee Pedersen, an Aquebogue man. O'Mahony was found guilty of fatally shooting Pedersen in a plot to steal his property.

Judge Mazzei arraigned Allen Case in October 2024 on charges of first-degree murder of an East Quogue man, underscoring the judge's role in significant criminal proceedings.

"Judge Mazzei will expect that we will conduct ourselves with the utmost professionalism during our press conference," Jayson said.

"As you know, we are seasoned at holding press conferences for high-profile cases, and Mac is the ultimate professional, as she served as a prosecutor for years," John said.

"I have watched Mac in action multiple times," Jayson said with a certain flee in his eyes, "And I know she knows what to do."

"We will follow your leadership," Mac suggested to Jayson. "You remain at the helm, and we serve as backup for any additional information to support you."

"Thank you. Are you ready to head over to the courthouse now?" John asked.

They shook their heads in unison. John was dressed in his FBI approved navy suit with a navy tie. Jayson was dressed in black slacks, a white button-down shirt and a sports coat. Mac, per her professional norm, wore her navy suit, navy heels and a cream-colored blouse with her long wavy auburn hair loosely tucked back behind her ears. All three had reading glasses dangling on a chain and carried briefcases.

Jayson hailed a cab and they were off, on their way to the Suffolk County Courthouse. There was already a crowd of people gathered, with news reporters, spectators and likely victims' families of the Gilgo murders. This was going to be a big day for them, and they knew that they would need to do a thorough and professional job updating the media and spectators with up-to-date information on these heinous crimes.

Jayson was the first to clip on his microphone and commence the press conference. He deftly informed the crowd on recent developments with the media coverage. John was next up with an update regarding the FBI and local law enforcement developments. Mac was last to the podium to help explain the legalities of the case and what she predicted to be the criminal trial procedures, including discovery, pre-trial conferences, and the projected setting on the trial date. She predicted that the case would go to trial in mid-June, 2025, and likely take three weeks for the trial. She also believed that Judge Mazzeo would allow the jury to deliberate as long as they needed and that a verdict would be rendered in short order based on the strength of the evidence. She then proceeded to inform the crowd that she believed that the judge would set the sentencing hearing within a week of the verdict.

At the end of the press conference, they answered questions from the audience before heading back to the hotel to get back to work.

"May I go with you to your war room in the hotel and further brainstorm with you regarding possible other victims?" Jayson asked while en route in the taxi.

"Of course, you may," John said. "We need all of the help that we can get."

"We work better as a team," Mac agreed. "John and I have consulted with many people on many cases, and we are better when we put our heads together and brainstorm with anyone who can add to our investigation."

"Thank you. I've never been invited to brainstorm with the FBI before, and I am thrilled for this opportunity," Jayson said.

"We are thrilled to have an investigative reporter and journalist on board. You likely see this case differently than we do," Mac said, secretly just wanting to spend more time with this gorgeous man. She felt tingly inside with his elbow touching hers.

John nudged her from the other side. He knew exactly what was going on. She gave John a side glance and he gave her one back. He was secretly hoping that Mac would fall in love again. He knew how hard she took the divorce from Burg. Burg was a good man, but he handled the Midnight Scribe and Tooth Fairy Killer cases very poorly and blamed her for endangering their family. He knew that Mac would never trust her ex-husband again.

When they returned to the hotel, they went their respective ways in order for Mac and John to change into something more comfortable before meeting Jayson in the war room to commence their brainstorming activity.

On the way down the hotel hall, John said to Mac, "I think you are slightly enamored with our resident journalist."

Mac let out a soft giggle when John gave her an affectionate nudge. "Whatever makes you think that?" she joked. "Is it my subtle flirting?"

"Not so subtle is more like it," John poked back. "You are about as subtle as thunder."

"Is it that obvious?"

"No, I am not sure he's picking up on it. I just know you well and I know when you have a man crush. Remember how you stumbled around that driver and bodyguard in the Tooth Fairy case? It's like that. Not obvious to others, but crystal clear to me," John said.

"Well, I will tone it down, as we need to remain professional during the investigation," Mac said.

"You are too old to be toning anything down. You're not a spring chicken anymore. You don't have the luxury of time. Don't take offense to that. And you both have a lot in common from being from the Wild West, to intelligence, to charm, to looks, to wit, and you both like to take on a challenge. Don't waste this. And you are only here a few more days before you need to go back to Wyoming and be with your kids. This is your first time away from them in years. You need to focus on your romantic life now. It's no fun to be alone. One day the four kids will be off in college and they won't need you as much, and you don't want to grow old alone. It's unhealthy."

"Thanks, Dad," Mac joked. But she knew deep down that he was right.

Chapter 7

"Let's discuss our known victims before we pivot to potential other victims," John said after the three of them settled in the war room. "The 'Gilgo Four' as our FBI task force refers to them have commonalities. Shanna Gilbert's disappearance in 2010 led to the discovery of the Gilgo Four. Her body was later found in a marsh near Oak Beach. Though her death was ruled as possibly accidental, her family believed she was murdered. Given the proximity to other victims, some speculated that Heuermann was involved," John said.

"Jessica Taylor's dismembered remains were found in Manorville in 2003, with additional remains discovered near Gilgo Beach in 2011," Jayson added. "Her case fits the pattern of dismemberment, which is present in some Gilgo cases."

"Valerie Mack was known and Jane Doe No., 6 for a while," John continued. "Like Taylor Mac's dismembered remains were found in Manorville in 2000, with her other parts discovered near Gilgo Beach in 2011. The timeline and disposal method suggests a potential link to the killer."

"The 'Fire Island Jane Doe' remains a mystery," Jayson continued. "Partial remains were found on Fire Island in 1996, with additional remains linked to her discovered near Gilgo Beach in 2011. The long timeframe between her disappearance and the discovery of her remains raises questions about the killer's activity over decades."

"Let's not forget 'Peaches and her child,'" Mac chimed in. "'Peaches is an unidentified woman whose torso was found in Hempstead Lake State Park in 1977. A child's remains, genetically linked to Peaches, were found near Gilgo Beach in 2011. The dumping of multiple victims with shared traits in the area raised the possibility of one killer."

"There are reports of missing women, primarily sex workers, who disappeared in the 1990s and 2000s in Long Island and nearby areas," Jayson added. "Heuermann's alleged targeting of sex workers might link him to additional unsolved cases."

"Additional unidentified remains, including a male victim and an Asan female, were found near Gilgo Beach. These cases remain unsolved but could be connected to Heuermann," John said.

"From my standpoint," Mac interjected, "Some victims were dismembered, while others were buried intact. The long gaps between some of the murders suggest the possibility of more victims or multiple killers. We have diverse M.O.s and a long timeline. I'm guessing that there are dozens of other victims out there that we have yet to discover."

"That's the fear from the FBI's perspective," John said.

"That is the fear of the entire community," Jayson said.

"I imagine that this is the fear from a lot of folks who live on Long Island," Mac said.

Both gentlemen shook their heads affirmatively, yet in silence.

Chapter 8

The next morning the headline feature was Jayson's story entitled "Gilgo Beach Murders Continued to Puzzle Investigators" and it was an eloquent statement of facts and opinions.

"The Gilgo Beach murders have puzzled investigators for over a decade, largely because of the variety of remains found in the area, which suggests either a highly adaptable killer or multiple killers, Shannan Gilvert was a 24-year-old sex worker who disappeared in May 2010 after running through Oak Beach, screaming for help. Her disappearance prompted the search that uncovered the "Gilgo Four.' Her body was found in a marshy area a year later. Her death was officially ruled as likely accidental drowning, but an independent autopsy suggested possible strangulation. Some believe she encountered Heuermann, or another killer that night."

The article continued. "Jessica Taylor was 20 when she disappeared in 2003. Her dismembered torso was found in Manorville, and her skull, hands, and forearm were found near Gilgo Beach in 2011. Jessica was a known sex worker. The precision of her dismemberment suggests a killer with anatomical knowledge. Manorville is near Heuermann's home in Massapequa Park, linking him geographically to her death. The use of multiple dump sites might indicate the same killer across the years, using Gilgo Beach as a 'final resting place.'"

"Valerie Mac was a 24-year-old sex worker and was last seen in 2000. Her torso was found in Manorville, with additional remains at Gilgo Beach. Like Jessica Taylor, her dismemberment showed careful planning and execution. The dumping of remains in two locations might signal Heuermann testing disposal methods or attempting to confuse investigators."

"The Fire Island Jane Doe remains were found in 1966 on Fire Island, with additional parts linked to her discovered at Gilgo Beach in 2011. The gap in time between discoveries suggests a killer revisiting the site or keeping remains as trophies. Heuermann may have been active much earlier than the 'Gilgo Four' indicating a long timeline of killings."

"Peaches and her child both remain unidentified. Peaches were found in Hempstead Lake State Park in 1977, marked by a distinctive tattoo of peaches, Her child's remains were later found at Gilgo Beach. The discovery of a mother and child suggests the killer may have killed them together or separately but used Gilgo Beach as a disposal ground for both. The emotional intensity of killing a child suggests the killer might have been escalating in violence or acting out in rage. The connection between dump sites might indicate a single killer's evolving methods. "

"The unidentified male and Asian female were both found among the Gilgo remains. The male was likely transgender, wearing women's clothing. The Asian female died of blunt force trauma. These victims deviate slightly from the pattern of young, white sex workers. The inclusion of these victims suggests the killer was targeting marginalized individuals possibly experimenting with victims outside the usual profile. Alternatively, they could be victims of a different killer who used the same area for disposal."

"Heuermann's proximity to Long Island, his meticulous behavior, and his alleged targeting of sex workers align with the patterns seen in the Gilgo Beach case. Theories suggest he began killing as early as the 1990s and adapted his methods over time, from dismemberment (Jessica Taylor and Valerie Mack) to whole-body burials (Gilgo Four)."

"The varying methods of body disposal (whole bodies, dismembered remains) and victim profiles (man, women, and children) lead some to believe there could be multiple killers using the same dumping ground. This theory gains traction from the length of time between some murders and the differences in M.O. Some speculate that the murder could be tied to a sex-trafficking ring or even multiple killers connected through organized crime. The deliberate place of bodies along Gilgo Beach could have symbolic or ritualistic meaning."

"If Heuermann is the sole killer, the differences in M.O. could show his progression from experimenting with dismemberment to refined disposal methods to avoid detection. He could have started as early as the 1990s, refining his tactics over the years."

"The investigation challenges remain consistent, there is a lack of victim identification as several remains are still unidentified, making it difficult to establish connections between victims. The widespread locations (Manorville, Hempstead, Fire Island, Gilgo Beach) complicate linking a single killer. The murders span decades with some victims killed years apart making the time gaps questionable."

"No matter how you slice it, the Gilgo Beach murders are terrifying."

Authors Note: I would like to cast a heartfelt nod of appreciation in writing this article to FBI profilers John Douglas and Mary MacIntosh. They have invited me into their inner circle and have shared information that this investigative reporter would not have had access to. It has helped me craft this informative piece.

Chapter 9

The next morning when John and Mac united in the war room, Jayson was waiting with a copy of his article for each of them to read. He watched them read his piece in the New York Times with great anxiety, as he was concerned that he might have shared FBI information that neither of them would have wanted them to share, but he was desperate for a juicy story as he had not written one in a bit. His boss was displeased with the lack of depth of his investigative reporting as of late. When Mac put down her newspaper, he waited for her to consult with John before speaking.

"I hope I didn't cross any professional boundaries with this piece," Jayson said, in an almost apologetic tone.

Mac was the first to speak. "Jayson, I think the article is intelligent and masterful, and I think the more the public knows about this case the better. My only concern is the multiple suggestions that this could be the work of multiple killers, as this is excellent legal fodder for Heuermann's defense team."

"I concur with counsel," John joined in. "Otherwise, I find it informative and well stated."

"I understand your concern, and I strongly considered it when crafting this, but it remains an obvious possibility, and the defense team must already be aware of this strategy," Jayson said, almost defensively.

"Let's move on. After you left to write this, John and I had some breakthroughs that we would love to share with you. The caveat is that you can't write about these yet. We need more time to explore."

"Understood and agreed," Jayson said with a sense of relief in his voice.

John pointed to the storyboard that Mac had created the night prior. "Massapequa Park is where we begin. Heuermann lived and worked here, within a short distance of both Gilgo Beach and Manorville. Manhattan is next. Heuermann worked as an architect in New York City. Unsolved murders of sex workers and missing persons in the 1990s and 2000s could be tied to him if he lured victims during trips between Long Island and the city. So last night we started examining cold cases. The Long Island Serial Killer or 'LISK' contains the 'Gilgo Four' and other bodies found along Ocean Parkway (Jessica Taylor, Valerie Mack, Peaches), etc. Heuermann fits the profile as he was a local with a steady career, familiarity with the area, and a lifestyle that could facilitate long-term killings. Add to the mix is unsolved Manhattan sex workers as victims in the late 1990s and early 2000s including many sex workers, often dismembered or strangled. Heuermann's professional presence in Manhattan during this time aligns with these cases."

Mac stood up with her laser point that she used to use in trials. "Let's turn to the Atlantic City Murders in 2006.

Four sex workers found in a drainage ditch behind a motel in Egg Harbor Township, New Jersey were all found face-down, barefoot, and positioned in a similar manner, echoing the M.O. seen in the Gilgo Beach murders. These are Green River Killer-style cases. Several women went missing in Connecticut, Rhode Island, and New Jersey between the 1980s and early 2000s. If Heuermann was active earlier, these cases might show his early experimentation before developing a consistent M.O."

John stood with his wooden pointing stick and pointed to Mac's storyboard. "Heuermann allegedly used burner phones to contact victims. A forensic analysis of his phone records will likely reveal patterns of movement matching crime scene locations, communication with other potential victims, and GPS pings of triangulation placing him near known or unsolved murder sites. Add to this Heuermann's DNA that has already been linked to the Gilgo Beach murders such as hair found on victims, combined with the recent court order for the cheek swap. If we anticipate what the FBI anticipates, re-testing DNA from cold cases, especially those involving unidentified remains, could match his profile. Advanced techniques like familial DNA searches for genealogy databases could link Heuermann to crimes further back in time."

Mac stood again. "His digital footprint would then be admissible in evidence at trial Evidence of searches for pornography, sex workers, or violent fantasies could align with profiles. Records of tools or items such as rope, tape, or other ligatures associated with crime scenes might tie him to specific methods of killing.

And let's not forget that many victims were sex workers, often petite, with histories of transient lifestyles. Bodies were dumped in isolated areas accessible to someone familiar with Long Island's geography. The methods of strangulation or dismemberment suggest control and planning."

John stood again. "Some victims deviate from this pattern, including males or children. This may indicate that Heuermann experimented with his victim profile or that some remains belong to a different killer. Mac is convinced that a further search warrant of his home on Long Island will reveal souvenirs or trophies from victims, tools matching marks on dismembered remains, and maps or notes showing premeditation of disposal sites. She has convinced the FBI to get a more specific search warrant of his home, and we are awaiting the judge to grant us the opportunity."

Mac remained sitting but with her psychology master's degree intact. "Heuermann fits a classic organized offender profile. He is intelligent, methodological, and living a double life. This is much like Ted Bundy, Rodney Alcala, and the Tooth Fairy Killer. Rex Heuermann had stable employment as an architect, hiding predatory behavior. This aligns with other long-term serial killers like Dennis Rader who was known as the BTK killer with similar traits. If Heuermann is connected to earlier cases, his progression may reflect increased confidence and refinement over time. Alternatively, if there are gaps in activity, he may have stopped temporarily due to personal reasons connected to his marriage, profession, or family obligations."

Jayson was taking this in, He'd never had the privilege of so much intelligent information gathering in his professional career.

John picked up where Mac left off. "The FBI is comparing the profiles of missing or murdered women across the Northeast in the 1990s through 2010s to Heuermann's known patterns. Serial killers often extend beyond their immediate area. Cases from Connecticut, New Jersey, and Pennsylvania are being reviewed as we speak. And we are testing evidence from older crime scenes with modern DNA techniques and this might produce matches."

"I know that I cannot share this in any investigatory article for the New York Times, but I am grateful for the opportunity to see your work in action," Jayson said. "I've never had the privilege to see the inner workings of the FBI."

"We are an unusual team, Mac and me. She offers legal and psychological input and I have access to all of the DNA and team, and together with her on our team as a consultant, we have solved a number of high-profile cases in just the last few years. You are watching her change the course of history with her immaculate storyboards and her dedication to rarely sleeping. I go to bed by 11 and wake up to a war room that is clean, organized, and full of new information. I don't know how she operates so well on so little sleep."

Mac guffawed at the notion. "You know that I had two sets of twins in three years, John. You were there to see the chaos and my tears and my filthy house, and my disheveled appearance! You know that I thrive in chaos."

John laughed at her. He adored her. Jayson simply looked confused.

Chapter 10

After Jayson left to report to the New York Times, John and Mac got back to work focusing on neighboring cases and possible links to Rex Heuermann and Gilgo Beach murder. They discovered that the Atlantic City Murders in 2006 might have a link. Four sex workers were found face-down in a drainage ditch behind the Golden Key Motel. Their shoes and socks were removed, and their heads were facing east. This was similar to Gilgo Beach. This targeted sex workers, specific victim positioning and ritualistic aspects. The proximity to New York made this a plausible connection. The next steps would include a comparison of DNA from the Atlantic City crime scenes to Heuermann's profile and to analysis of travel records to see if Heuermann visited Atlantic City.

The Manorville Murders of the 1990s and 2000s were an obvious fit and Rex Heuermann had already been indicted for these.

Other unsolved New York City and Long Island cases of missing and murdered sex workers in this timeframe would need to be considered.

DNA evidence would be key. Investigators had already linked Heuermann to the Gilgo Beach murders via a female hair found on one victim's body, identified as likely belonging to Heuermann's wife.

The next step would be to re-test evidence from other cold cases using advanced methods like DNA phenotyping or genealogy databases. The criminologists would need to perform Y-STR testing to track male-specific DNA markers in unsolved cases.

Geographic profiling was next on Mac and John's list. They wanted GIS mapping to analyze dump site patterns including the proximity to Heuermann's home or office. They wanted to seek out his routes for commuting.

 Heuermann's burner phones needed to be linked to current technology, in Mac's opinion. They sought to recover the burner phones that he used to contact sex workers. Mac wanted to cross-reference these burner phone records with police databases to match him to other victims.

John noted that many of the victims in the Gilgo Beach case remained unidentified. He wanted to use advanced forensic genealogy to reveal connections to known missing persons. With this, they could test remains for any familial DNA matches and compare timelines to Heuermann's movements.

Mac was glued to the psychological aspects of Rex Heuermann. She was fixated on his organized planning and his disorganized execution of crimes. She knew that Jayson also had a master's degree in psychology, so they invited him back for further brainstorming on the psychology of a serial killer.

Chapter 11

When Jayson arrived the next day at the war room, he brought good coffee, bagels with locks and cream cheese with fresh chives from his garden, and fresh tomatoes that he grew. He made John and Mac a masterful bagel and presented them with a home-cooked meal. This was highly unusual and breathtakingly wonderful.

John took the helm to continue the discussion. But it was not lost on him that Jayson had gone to the trouble of bringing them a home-grown breakfast. Men didn't do this for other men. This was directed at Mac. And it was romantic and adorable to John.

John and Jayson both watched Mac devour her food. She was tall and fit and thin, but she ate like she was starving at all times. It was endearing to some. It was annoying to others. It appeared to be endearing to Jayson. John took notice.

"It's our last day with Mac, so we need to take advantage of it. She heads back tomorrow morning to Sheridan, Wyoming to take care of her four kids next week. We need to get started."

"Four kids?" Jayson said. "Holy cow. You don't look like you have had a child. I have two kids and my ex-wife looks like she's been through the wringer."

"Mac had two sets of twins in two years. She cried about it. Don't get her started," John joked.

"She's a great mom, and she shares custody every other week, so we have her every other week in New York until we can solve the Gilgo Beach case, so let's make the most of our last day together."

Mac stood. "Let's talk about the dichotomy of this man. He is a very organized killer in that he has a stable family life and a career as a cover. He has a methodical approach to selecting victims and dumping bodies. He uses burner phones to avoid detection. However, the mix of dismemberment and intact bodies suggests experimentation or shifting methods over time."

John took over. "The potential motives baffle the FBI. Heuermann's alleged targeting of vulnerable sex workers points to a need for domination. And we see some symbolism in the dump sites. Gilgo Beach as a common disposal site might reflect a personal or ritualistic attachment. If we can connect the earlier dismemberment cases, Heuermann may have evolved to quicker, more efficient disposal methods, such as burying intact bodies."

"There are many behavioral red flags," Mac added. "Heuermann maintained the façade of a family man and professional architect, reminiscent of killers like Dennis Rader who was the BTK, or Israel Keyes. If trophies can be recovered from his home or office, it would suggest he relived the crimes. I have been delving into psychological drivers.

What I see is the potential for abandonment or childhood trauma. If these are present, they may be the factors that may explain why Heuermann allegedly chose women who might represent figures of past pain or rejection. And then I would like to explore a long cooling-off period or inconsistent killing pattern which might suggest external factors such as his marriage, children, or other influencing activities."

"The FBI is focused on re-testing cold case evidence and we are working with local law enforcement in this area to reopen unsolved cases in New York, New Jersey, and Connecticut from the 1990s-2010s to test for DNA and other physical evidence. We need to look for commonalities among missing sex workers or other unidentified remains within Heuermann's potential hunting grounds.

As they worked into the late afternoon, John announced that it was time that he took his train back to his family in D.C., leaving Jayson alone with Mac.

"Do you want to grab dinner on your last night in the city?" he asked with a certain feeling of self-doubt and loathing. He felt like he was over his skis in asking.

"I would love to," Mac said. "I've barely left this hotel in Times Square since I arrived, and I have never been to New York."

"You have got to be kidding me," he said. "Did you bring smart clothing for a night on the town?"

"I did! I have not done anything fun in so long, other than with the kids."

"I'll go home and change, and I'll pick you up at eight. I'll get a reservation before a Broadway show. I'll see if I can snag any last-minute tickets."

Mac had never been to a Broadway show. She was excited.

When he showed up looking very dapper in dating clothes, reservations to a posh restaurant on Broadway, and tickets to WICKED, she could not believe it. Mac had never been to a Broadway show, and the performances were extraordinary. She felt like she was floating six feet above him.

They had the time of their lives. They woke up in her hotel room late, and she almost missed her flight home!

Chapter 12

Mac got back to Sheridan on the late flight and was excited to attend mass with her children the following evening. The four kids were happy to be back with their mom, as they hadn't seen her for a week, which was very unusual.

Mac realized that taking a little time to herself was good for everyone, as it appeared that the kids appreciated her a tad more. But she also missed Jayson. Sleeping in his arms was heavenly. Being that he was two hours ahead of her in time zones, she woke up daily to a lovely text from him wishing her good morning with a kiss emoji. It surprised her how much this meant to her. She had never been the recipient of an emoji from a man, and it felt heartfelt and genuine.

She returned the text message with a thoughtful note and an emoji as well, and this was their pattern for the week that she was back in Wyoming. He even offered to fly to see her that week, but she explained on a phone call that she needed to focus on her kids in the weeks that she was with them and reminded him that she would be back in New York on Sunday night.

Chapter 13

When Mac arrived back in New York, Jayson volunteered to pick her up at JFK and drive her to the hotel to meet up with John in the war room for a quick debriefing before a nightcap. They would need to regroup early Monday morning and get cracking on the Gilgo Beach murders. John had kept Mac up to speed via emails and telephone calls when she was in Sheridan, Wyoming, but he had not touched the storyboard. That was Mac's domain, and John knew better than to mess with perfection. Her storyboards told a crime investigation like no other. The FBI staff took notes and would stop by the war room just to see her creations.

When Mac and Jayson turned in for the night, they decided to just talk about the status of their relationship and where they thought it was going.

"I need to disclose to you that I struggle with vulnerability after past losses, and I am challenged with balancing my professional drive with personal happiness. It was part of the cause of my divorce with Burg," she confessed.

"I understand completely. My professional drive is part of the cause of my divorce as well," Jayson admitted. "Her infidelity did not help matters either."

Mac was unaware of his relationship with his ex-wife and could only imagine what it must feel like to be married to an unfaithful spouse. She and Burg had their differences, but neither of them had ever been unfaithful.

The deception and pain and lack of trust moving forward had to be an imminent threat. She was unsure as to how far to go in that discussion so early in their relationship and decided to let him unfold this information on his terms.

"Prepare yourself for my guilt of feeling torn between my consulting work in New York and my responsibilities as a mother in Wyoming. My kids will struggle with my absence, and I will face criticism from other parents and from Burg about prioritizing my career over my family."

"I receive similar criticism regarding my prioritization of my career, not only from my ex but also from other parents. My two children are of similar age to yours, and they are slightly outspoken teenagers about my work ethic," Jayson admitted.

"Tell me about your two kids?" Mac asked. "I've told you about my twins over a few telephone calls, but you haven't said much about your children."

"They are typical self-absorbed teenagers. Clayton is sixteen and can now drive, but I would not recommend that you get in a car when he is behind the wheel. And Angelica is 14 and a high school soccer player and she is badass. She flattens opponents and I must admit, she's so fun to watch play, but I would hate to see this tall glass of water coming at me on the field at full speed ahead. She celebrates her goals in such a ridiculous fashion that it is a tad embarrassing," Jayson said. "Clayton is no better on the tennis court. He loves to ace his serves and fist pumps in celebration almost every time."

Mac giggled in response. She had disclosed how athletic her four kids were and relentless about victory.

"If we pursue this relationship, our kids will meet each other and the six of them could gang up on us," Mac said with a twinkle in her eye. "My kids have met Burg's new love, and they seem to like her. I don't think they love that she moved in already though."

"I'm sure that it is weird to see your parents with another person, but it is inevitable," Jayson said.

"My ex has a new guy in her life, and they moved forward with cohabitation quickly and then remarriage. I think it was too soon for the kids, but the guy is a solid choice, and now I don't have to pay spousal support anymore, and I must admit that it's nice to have that money remain on my side of the balance sheet," Jayson said.

"I wish that Burg would marry his new leading lady. Then I would not have to pay him spousal support. I think he is not getting married just to spite me."

Jayson rolled his eyes. It had never dawned on him that spousal support is a two-way street.

"You are not going to believe this, but my kids know one of the children of one of our Gilgo Beach murder victims," Jayson said. "She goes to high school with them. Her mom was apparently a sex worker and had this girl out of wedlock as a teenager. She was adopted from a foster home as a little girl and is being raised in a nice home in a New York suburb, but I am sure that the nightly news regarding this case is not lost on her that her mother was murdered and dismembered by the accused Rex Heuermann," Jayson said.

Mac could only shake her head. She could only imagine the pain and suffering of a child to know that your mother died at the hands of a ruthless animal of a man.

"Is that something that you had to disclose to the New York Times as a potential conflict of interest?" Mac asked.

"Yes, it was something that I had to disclose, but I also made my boss promise that I did not have to write about it as part of my coverage of this story. I don't want to drag anyone's kids into this," Jayson said.

"Nor should you. Kids don't belong in the news unless it is good news," Mac said.

"Agreed."

Chapter 14

John and Jayson watched Mac update the storyboard as John continued to download them on what the FBI team had uncovered during Mac's absence.

"It appears that Rex Heuermann manipulated his wife's trips to make her an unwitting alibi, but she started to suspect something was wrong, which created tension in their marriage," John said.

"Do you think that his wife was complicit in these crimes?" Mac asked while continuing to update her storyboard.

"Well, I don't know if we can use the word complicit, but she certainly started to pick up on patterns, but she refuses to be a witness against her husband, likely out of fear that she could be charged with an accessory after the fact," John said.

"What about the kids? They were home when their father was out killing people. They had to have been curious about his absence from the home," Jayson said,

"Mac asked that our legal team serve them with written discovery last week after she had the opportunity to review and revise it. I am quite certain that Heuermann's legal defense team will be in court soon with a motion for a protective order regarding his adult kids, but I doubt that the judge will grant it They are not minors, and they should be called as witnesses in this trial," John said.

"The request for admissions is what I want most," Mac said. "I want these adult children to admit that they knew that their dad was out and about when they were minors, leaving them alone when their mother was out of town. And I believe that each murder likely took place near a significant architectural landmark tied to Rex's designs, and I think this will unveil additional victims that connect his professional life to his crimes."

"Mac suggested last week that Heuermann's children unknowingly hold vital information about his crimes such as uncovering possible 'souvenirs' that he brought home after these brutal murders. She thinks that the kids might have been too young at the time to relate his quirky disappearances in the night or the 'souvenirs,' but she thinks that her specifically worded discovery requests when answered, might uncover additional information about these crimes," John said.

Jayson's phone started buzzing in a crazy fashion. Within seconds, Mac and John's phones blew up as well. John turned on the television and they watched the breaking news.

A victim was found in an upscale brownstone under renovation, and the crime scene mimicked the layout of the home's blueprint, with the victim's body staged as though they were "part" of Rex's design. In addition, a cryptic symbol was etched into the floor and has been identified as a reference to an architectural feature from Heuermann's portfolio.

John turned to Mac and Jayson and studied the shocked look on both of their faces.

"You have got to be kidding me," Jayson said. "Mac, you called it. You foresaw this last week."

"She did. That's why we were able to get the search warrant for all of the buildings that he has worked on over the years. I think that more bodies will be unveiled," John said.

Just then, there was additional breaking news. Another body was discovered on the rooftop of a skyscraper that Rex helped design. The victim was posed as though she was "admiring" the view. The victim's phone contained an unsent text with coordinates to another building Rex worked on. Teams of law enforcement were scrambling to get to the next potential crime scene.

"This is insane," Jayson said.

"Heuermann is insane," Mac said. "He is mentally ill. Now I am worried that he will plead not guilty by means of insanity and never stand trial for these murders and be allowed to live out his life in a state psychiatry hospital."

"The judge won't stand for it, Mac, and you know it. This is not his first high-profile case, and the meticulous planning of these crimes as revealed on Heuermann's computer proves that he is not insane. The fact that he's a well-known architect also serves as proof that he is mentally fit to stand trial," John said.

All three of their phones blew up again. Another victim was just uncovered in an abandoned subway station, highlighting Heuermann's knowledge of New York's hidden infrastructure. The victim was found positioned near a forgotten architectural detail, symbolizing decay and neglect.

A piece of a blueprint was found on the victim, torn from one of Rex's past designs.

They watched this live television coverage of body after body being discovered on the same day. It was mind-blowing.

Chapter 15

Mac, John, and Jayson watched as law enforcement teams raced to discover the clue from the subway victim. The blueprint found on the victim was a piece of the design of a building where upscale New York City galas were often held. The blueprint has Heuermann's architectural firm RH Consultants & Associates stamp on the bottom, and it was the project where he was hired to renovate office and ballroom space in The Trump Building, a landmark property on Wall Street.

The Trump Building, located at 40 Wall Street in Manhattan's Financial District, is a 72-story neo-Gothic skyscraper standing 927 feet high. It was designed by architect H. Craig Severance with associate architect Yasuo Matsui and consulting architects Shreve & Lamb and was constructed between 1929 and 1930 as the headquarters for the Manhattan Company.

The building features a limestone façade on its lower levels, transitioning to buff-colored brick with numerous setbacks on the upper stories, culminating in a distinctive green pyramidal roof. Its design includes narrow vertical bays of windows, contributing to its slender appearance.

Originally known as the Manhattan Company Building, it briefly held the title of the world's tallest building before being surpassed by the Chrysler Building. In 1995, Donald

Trump acquired the building's leasehold and renamed it The Trump Building.

Today, 40 Wall Street offers approximately 1.3 million square feet of Class-A office space, with floor plans ranging from 6,000 to 38,000 square feet. Tenants enjoy 360-degree unobstructed city and water views, along with high-quality management and concierge services.

Law enforcement raced to The Trump Building's main ballroom to find yet another victim of Rex Heuermann staged as though she was enjoying city and water views.

The three of them stared at the television in total disbelief. Mac was the first to break the silence.

"Rex Heuermann's dual life as a family man and serial killer obviously stems from deep psychological scars. His meticulousness and charm masked a fractured persona. I think that we are going to unearth a man who was raised in a controlling household with a domineering parent, and this helped develop his sense of perfectionist tendencies to cope. I believe that he resents his mother for stifling his individuality, fueling a subconscious desire to dominate and control others," she said.

"Architecture represents control and permanence to him," John continued. "His killings reflect his need to 'design' his victims' final moments as though they're part of his creations."

"Agreed," Mac said. "Each murder scene mimics architectural principles – symmetry, balance, or even chaos, reflecting his mental state at the time.

To maintain his family façade, he compartmentalized his life, creating rigid mental 'blueprints' for how he should act. His wife and children serve as the 'foundation' of his stability, but her absences trigger his darker impulses."

"Heuermann is driven by a craving for acknowledgment – not as a family man or an architect but as an artist of death," Jayson suggested. "Leaving cryptic symbols at each scene is his way of signing his 'work,' challenging law enforcement to uncover his identity."

'That is insightful," Mac said, acknowledging that Jayson also held a master's degree in psychology.

"The fact of the matter is that we had a madman on the loose in my city, and I am grateful that he is behind bars," Jayson said.

"The terrifying fact that still exists is that I believe that we are not finished uncovering further victims," Mac said.

"Yes," John agreed. "This is a stay-tuned moment in history."

Chapter 16

It was not long after the written discovery was served on Heuermann's adult children, and the judge denied the protective order that Rex Heuermann entered a guilty plea to all charges of murder.

Mac, John, and Jayson attended the sentencing hearing wherein the judge ordered him to serve a life sentence without the possibility of parole. The prosecutor was wise to not seek the death penalty, and the plea did not allow for appeals.

Rex Heuermann would go down in history as the Gilgo Beach Killer and would be held responsible for murdering dozens of people in New York.

Chapter 17

"I am grateful that this investigation is over," Mac said to John and Jayson back at the hotel restaurant where they would share their last meal together before Mac needed to fly back to Wyoming the next morning. "However, I will miss working with you two."

"There will be more cases, Mac," John said reassuringly. "And I doubt that it is the last time you two will see each other."

"Absolutely not!" Jayson exclaimed. "I'm flying to Sheridan tomorrow with Mac. She's going to introduce me to her family."

John's eyes grew wide with excitement and hope. "That's great news. She should not be alone. She's fiercely independent, but she's also a devout partner. You deserve one another."

"Thank you," Mac said as tears welled in her eyes. She raised her glass of champagne, and they toasted their future together.

"Cheers," they said in unison.

www.ingramcontent.com/pod-product-compliance
Lightning Source LLC
Chambersburg PA
CBHW030838070225
21319CB00002B/79

* 9 7 9 8 3 4 8 4 7 0 3 5 7 *